Dear Reader

I have loved reading sinc̲e̲ ̲ ̲ ̲ ̲ ̲ ̲ ̲ ̲ ̲ ̲
books have always been my ̲ ̲ ̲ ̲ ̲ ̲ scape!

When I write stories about Ugenia, I feel
like I'm going on a fantastic adventure. I start
with an idea . . . and I never know how it's going
to end until I get there. It's like Ugenia
Lavender has a life of her own and I get lost in
Ugenia's world, where anything can happen!

Ugenia's friends and family are all people
we'd recognize in our own lives, and I hope
all readers, young and old, will have fun with
Ugenia and all her friends.

Ugenia is both flawed and inspirational – she
sometimes acts up, and isn't afraid to ask for
what she wants, but when she fails at anything
she tries again, and always with a big smile!
Perhaps Ugenia Lavender is a bit like me – or
maybe even you!

I hope you grow to love her as much as I do.

Geri xx

Geri Halliwell shot to fame with the Spice Girls, a global music phenomenon selling over 55 million CDs.

She has travelled extensively as a United Nations Goodwill Ambassador with particular interest in issues affecting women and children, and she has had two bestselling autobiographies published.

Geri lives in London and has a daughter, Bluebell Madonna.

Books by Geri Halliwell

Ugenia Lavender

Ugenia Lavender and the Terrible Tiger

Ugenia Lavender and the Burning Pants

Ugenia Lavender: Home Alone

Ugenia Lavender and the Temple of Gloom

Ugenia Lavender: The One and Only

uGenia Lavender

inspirational!

impossible!

love it!

Ugenia Lavender

Home Alone

Geri Halliwell

Illustrated by Rian Hughes

MACMILLAN CHILDREN'S BOOKS

This is a work of fiction. These stories, characters, places and events are all completely made-up, imaginary and absolutely not true.

Ugenia Lavender X

First published 2008 by Macmillan Children's Books

This edition published 2009 by Macmillan Children's Books
a division of Macmillan Publishers Limited
20 New Wharf Road, London N1 9RR
Basingstoke and Oxford
Associated companies throughout the world
www.panmacmillan.com

ISBN 978-0-330-45431-5

Text and illustrations copyright © Geri Halliwell 2008
Illustrations by Rian Hughes
Brain Squeezers by Amanda Li

The right of Geri Halliwell to be identified as the
author of this work has been asserted by her in accordance with the
Copyright, Designs and Patents Act 1988.

1 3 5 7 9 8 6 4 2

A CIP catalogue record for this book is available from
the British Library.

Printed and bound in the UK by CPI Mackays, Chatham ME5 8TD

Contents

To Bluebell. Little girl, big imagination.

1

uGenia Lavender

Get Me Out of Here!

Ugenia woke up one sparkly Tuesday
morning. The sun was ready for action and
it was the holidays. No school – cool!

But there was something that was weird
about Ugenia this morning. There was no
enthusiastic leap out of bed, no mission-
impossible plans to make and definitely
no toothpaste-advert smile in the mirror.
Instead she slumped to the floor, practically
rolled to the bathroom and stared at her

face in the mirror. It stared back at her saying, 'I'M BORED . . .'

Ugenia went downstairs and wandered through the house, picking up books she'd already read, flicking channels on the TV and staring into the fridge. 'Boring!' she sighed. 'My life is boring, boring, borrrrrrrrring – nothing exciting ever happens here.'

'Why don't you come shopping with me?' said her mum, Pandora Lavender, who had just got back from her work as a presenter on Breakfast TV.

'Shopping's boring,' said Ugenia glumly.

'I'm going to inspect some dinosaur poo
– you can come with me!' said her dad,
Professor Lavender, who was a specialist in
pretty much everything and worked at the
Dinosaur Museum in town.

'Boring,' said Ugenia. 'I guess I'll just
see what Rudy's up to. Maybe he's doing
something exciting.'

Ugenia hopped on her red bike and
cycled over to Rudy's house. Rudy lived
two streets away on Leavesden Road where
all the houses were stuffed together like
cheese-and-pickle sandwiches. Rudy lived
right on the corner above his dad's shop,
Patels' Food Store, except it didn't only
sell food, it sold newspapers, Sellotape and
weird things like pliers.

But the most distinct thing about Rudy's

home was the fantastic smell of his mum's cooking. She often had a large pot of curry on the stove, which always smelt delicious.

Ugenia liked Rudy's mum, Rifat Patel, a lot, as she always gave Ugenia interesting food – like lamb curry with coconut naan bread – whenever she came over, even if it wasn't lunchtime.

'Hello, Ugenia,' said Rifat now. 'Rudy is upstairs watching a movie. Why don't you take up these onion bhajis for a snack? I've just made them.'

'Cool, thanks,' said Ugenia. Now *these* don't look boring! she thought.

Rudy was in his room, staring transfixed at the TV.

'Rudy, you're so lucky,' Ugenia sighed. 'Your family's really fantastic and

interesting. I'm so bored with everything in my life – nothing ever happens and there's never anything to do.'

'Watch this,' replied Rudy, not taking his eyes off the TV. 'It's a Hunk Roberts movie called *Gorillas in the Mud*.'

Ugenia stared at the screen at her favourite action hero, Hunk Roberts, as he danced with large gorillas in a jungle.

'Wow,' gasped Ugenia, 'that looks far more exciting than living in Cromer Road.'

Rudy's mum came in then, bringing Ugenia and Rudy a large glass of tarberry juice each. She sat down with them and began to comb her long hair that had never been cut.

'Ugenia, Rudy's father and I were discussing how nice it would be if you could come on holiday to India with the three of us,' she said. 'We're going next week.'

'INCREDIBLE!' screamed Ugenia in excitement. 'I would love to!'

'Well, India's beautiful – there are golden beaches and amazing people, but you must ask your parents first, obviously,' said Rifat.

Ugenia leaped up, gabbling that she had

to get home immediately. She tore down the stairs, flung open the front door and jumped on her bike, pedalling as fast as she could back home to 13 Cromer Road.

'Mum! Dad!' she yelled as she ran into the house. 'I've been asked to go on holiday with the Patels to India! Can I go? It's going to be amazing!' And Ugenia hopped

up and down like an electric kangaroo on super-charged batteries.

'Er, I'm sorry, Ugenia, but no, you can't go,' said her mum.

'It's just not possible,' said her dad.

'INJUSTICE!' screamed Ugenia. 'That's so unfair – you never let me do anything!'

'It's just that we have our own family holiday planned,' said Professor Lavender gently. 'It was going to be a big surprise.'

'Really?' frowned Ugenia. 'Where?'

'Lamorca – it's a Spanish island,' said Pandora, smiling.

'I don't wanna go to Spain – that's boring!' said Ugenia, scowling. How could anywhere possibly be as exciting as India?

'Actually, Lamorca has a lot of history,' said Professor Lavender. 'There are all sorts

of prehistoric myths and legends about
the island. It's apparently the place where
the first Gorillasaurus rex lived, over two
million years ago. The Gorillasaurus was
bigger than a house, bigger than a T. rex.
In fact, it was absolutely GINORMOUS.'

Boring, thought Ugenia gloomily. Seen
it, done it and bought the T-shirt.

'Ugenia, you should try to enjoy the fact
that next week you're going on a holiday
with your *own* family,' said Pandora firmly.
'We've been promised a great package – a
three-star hotel, entertainment and meals
included.'

'It will be great fun! There'll be your
mum, Granny Betty, your Uncle Harry and
me!' said her dad, smiling enthusiastically.

Boring, thought Ugenia again. 'Nothing

exciting ever happens in my life – it's all BORING!' she huffed, stomping upstairs and slamming her bedroom door, which made the house tremble.

The following week the Lavender family was packed and ready to go. They whizzed off to the airport in a big taxi and boarded the Squeezy Jet plane. It was all a bit of a scramble as everyone squashed into their seats and the packed aircraft took off into the sky towards sunny Spain. Uncle Harry sat with Professor Lavender, Granny Betty sat with Pandora, and Ugenia sat next to a very, very stinky fat lady who was sweating a lot and took up half Ugenia's seat as well as her own.

'I'm afraid there's no room in the

overhead compartment for this,' said a
rather flustered and snooty flight attendant
as she handed back Ugenia's luminous
yellow rucksack as if it smelt.

'But I have no space myself!' said Ugenia
with her knees squashed up to her chin.

'This plane food is dreadful!' said Uncle
Harry, accidentally elbowing Professor
Lavender in the head.

11

'There's no room for my vanity case,' sighed Pandora.

'These mini rolls are yummy,' said Granny Betty.

'Have you read the safety instructions?' said Professor Lavender, peering in the rack in front of him.

Boring, thought Ugenia.

Ugenia was so bored she tried a few things to help pass the time – flicking peanuts over the seat at the passengers' heads in front of her then pretending to be asleep when they turned around, blowing into the sick bag and then pretending to vomit, and finally trying to read the safety manual,

12

which was by far the most boring . . .

Finally, Ugenia decided the only thing for it was to take a trip to the loo and experiment with the handwipes and free cologne. After that she squeezed herself back into her seat next to the stinky fat lady, who was now fast asleep and drooling over Ugenia's luminous yellow rucksack.

One long hour and forty very boring minutes later, the Lavenders fastened their seat belts and descended with a bump on to the runway of Lamorca's little airport.

'Good afternoon, ladies and gentlemen. *¡Hola! ¡Buenas tardes!* Welcome to Lamorca,' said the pilot over the cabin radio.

'Thank goodness!' said Ugenia as she quickly jumped out of her seat and marched towards the exit doors.

After a long and boring wait in the passport line, and then a long and boring wait for all the Lavenders' mountain of luggage, they clambered into a dusty old minibus for the long ride out towards Palma Nova. Finally, they were dropped off at their three-star hotel and greeted by their hotel representative.

'Hello, everybody, my name is Coleen. Welcome to Palma Lamorca Hotel. Not only does your package include breakfast, lunch and dinner – we also have a magnificent swimming pool and evening entertainment!' She guided them into the

hotel reception and handed them all some
fruit punch. 'There's plenty to do and
see here. This afternoon we have aqua-
aerobics, and tonight there's a karaoke
competition and an eat-as-much-as-you-
like fish buffet,' Colleen added, smiling.

Ugenia rolled her eyes with boredom. So
this is what our holiday is going to be like

– boring fish and bad singing, she thought,
frowning.

☆

Over the next few days, the Lavenders'
holiday consisted of exactly that – lots of
aqua-aerobics in the pool, many fish buffets
and karaoke competitions, which all the
Lavenders joined in with enthusiastically,
except for Ugenia, who found everything
completely and utterly boring. She began to
moan profusely.

'I hate aqua-aerobics and fish buffets
and karaoke. They're all utterly boring,'
she said.

'I'm actually finding the fish buffets
rather inspirational,' said Uncle Harry, who
was a chef.

'I'm loving the karaoke,' said Granny

Betty, who had been a friend of a famous singer called Elvis when she was young, and who still liked to climb on the kitchen table and sing along with pop songs, even though she was 101 years old and should really know better.

'My tan is coming on a treat doing the aqua-aerobics!' said Ugenia's mum.

'Why don't you just try to enjoy it with the rest of us?' said her dad. But before Ugenia could tell them exactly why she found it all so dull, Colleen began the early evening announcements.

'Tomorrow we have something a bit different for all you more adventurous holidaymakers. We're going on an excursion!' she exclaimed. 'We shall be taking a boat trip to a mysterious and

ancient island of exotic spices and pirates.
It's a really wonderful place that is
completely uninhabited.'

'Fantastic!' said Professor Lavender.
'Right, Ugenia?'

'I suppose so. Anything is better than
aqua-aerobics,' grumbled Ugenia.

The next morning, at nine o'clock sharp,
the Lavender family boarded a glass-
bottomed boat with Colleen. They then
stopped off at another neighbouring island
and a large group of twenty-five German
people joined them, making the boat
extremely crowded.

'Ouch! Mind my foot, you oaf,' muttered
Uncle Harry to a large man who was
bright red from too much sunbathing.

Ugenia began to feel hot and flustered as she was squashed into the corner of the boat and the only thing she could see was a lady's sweaty, hairy armpit. 'Are we nearly there yet?' she huffed to her parents.

One very long hour later, just as Ugenia was about to explode with frustration, the glass-bottomed boat pulled up to a beautiful deserted island with a stretch of white sandy beach and a vast jungle with a mountain

range peering over top. The ocean glistened with crystal-clear water.

'We're here!' said Colleen as the Lavender family and the large bunch of Germans clambered on to the beach.

The mystery pirate-and-spice-island excursion consisted of most of the German holidaymakers, led by Uncle Harry,

assembling a huge barbecue and then roasting five large chickens, while the rest of the Lavenders fished for crabs and shellfish with a few of the German children. There was a bustle of activity on the beach as everyone seemed to be getting on marvellously, all except for Ugenia, who still felt extremely glum and bored.

'This isn't exactly exciting, is it? I thought there'd be some sort of adventure at least,' groaned Ugenia.

'Come and have some chicken and sauerkraut,' said Hans, a German holidaymaker who was trying to be friendly to Ugenia. 'I have plenty, come and join us. Or I have cheese and bratwurst,' he finished, offering her a large sausage.

'Thanks, but no thanks,' said Ugenia.

'Come and fish for a crab!' called Granny Betty.

'Let's tan together!' said her mother Pandora.

'Take a look at this marvellous mollusc specimen I found,' said her dad.

'Thanks, but no thanks,' replied Ugenia, who'd decided she wanted to be alone and wandered off down the beach. Everyone else was quite preoccupied with their own activities, so nobody noticed.

The sun was extremely hot as it beat down on the beach. Ugenia strolled in towards the jungle for some shade. Besides, she needed a wee, so she looked for somewhere private as she wandered further into the jungle.

Ugenia trudged a little deeper through

the lush glossy vines and thick trees until she came to a secluded spot.

Ah, this looks like a good spot, thought Ugenia as she removed her luminous yellow rucksack, pulled down her denim shorts and crouched behind a bush.

Ugenia took a long satisfying wee . . . 'Ah, that's so much better, I'm ready for some lunch now!' she said as she buttoned up her shorts then peered out above the bushes.

But as Ugenia scanned the jungle for the route she'd taken, she realized she had no idea where she was . . . or which was the

way back to her family and the Germans
on the beach . . . it all looked the same.
Ugenia had no idea how far she had come
into the jungle!

Crikey, what am I going to do? thought
Ugenia, who was trying not to get worried.
OK, I'll take a lucky guess . . . Ugenia
then spun round and decided just to walk
in a straight line towards what looked like
the friendliest route, with bushes that had
the least prickly, spiky leaves. She tried not
to freak out about all the strange noises
and rustles she kept on hearing. 'La la la,
everything is just fine, yes, la la la, it's all
fine,' she hummed to herself.

After twenty minutes of marching
vigorously, Ugenia was beginning to feel
rather tired. Then she saw a clearing ahead

of her . . . it was the beach!

Ugenia jumped for joy. 'I'm starving – I'm so hungry I could even eat some of that weird sauerkraut . . .'

As the jungle opened out on to the large stretch of white sand, Ugenia looked around for her family and the Germans . . . but there wasn't anybody in sight. She stared into the distance, but all she could see was mountains of jungle with a monumental volcano looming above them.

'Where is everyone? Have they left without me or is this a different place?' Ugenia asked herself.

Ugenia stared in disbelief. The beach was truly deserted – no Mum, no Dad, no Uncle Harry, no Granny Betty, no Germans, no roasting chicken, no sausage or cheese – no one. Just Ugenia, lost on a desert island.

'Well, I'm certainly alone now, aren't I?' She shrugged. 'Still, I suppose that at least I've got some space,' she said, trying to convince herself that she didn't feel scared. But Ugenia felt very scared.

She stared at the piercing blue sky. As the sun beat down on her, she could feel her skin begin to burn and beads of sweat began to roll down her face.

I'm thirsty, thought Ugenia, rummaging through her luminous rucksack, pulling out a plastic bottle and desperately drinking the last drop of tarberry juice.

'I'm hungry,' said Ugenia, nibbling a tiny crumb of bread roll and licking a fudge wrapper that she found at the bottom of her bag. 'What am I going to do? If I go back into the jungle I'm going to get even more lost. I'm going to starve to death! Help I need rescuing!' cried Ugenia, who felt pretty silly as no one could hear her. 'How will any one even know I'm here? It's not like I can make a phone call.'

Ugenia stared at the rest of the contents of her yellow rucksack: one Big News! diary, one pen, one pair of shades and one now empty tarberry-juice bottle.

'Not much use now,' said Ugenia, slinging the bottle on to the beach . . . when suddenly, like a thunderbolt of lightning, Ugenia had a brainwave.

'Ingenious!' she cried. 'A bottle message! If I write a message on this notepad and send it back to Britain, hopefully someone will find it.'

So Ugenia wrote:

SOS
STRANDED ON DESERT ISLAND
WITH NOTHING TO DO
I'M UGENIA LAVENDER,
GET ME OUT OF HERE↓

Ugenia screwed
the lid on tightly,
kissed the
bottle for
good luck
and threw it
as far out to sea
as she could.

Ugenia stared at the sun, the sun stared
at Ugenia and she began to melt.

'I'm so hungry!' said Ugenia, staring at a caterpillar.

'I'm so hot!'

'I'm so thirsty . . .'

'And there's no one around even to talk to,' frowned Ugenia. 'Isn't it the first sign of madness, when you start talking to yourself? Stop it!' she cried as something suddenly hit her on the head. 'Ouch!'

Ugenia turned to look at the offending object – a mouldy old football. 'Where on earth did that come from?'

'Oops, sorry, he's mine,' said a man wearing a tiny pair of undies, who was very skinny with a long beard. Nervously he snatched up the football and cradled it like a baby . . .

'Who are *you*?' frowned Ugenia, feeling

29

a mixture of annoyance and relief to see someone.

'Forgive me, I've forgotten my manners. My name's Forrest, and this is my friend Nelson,' exclaimed Forrest pointing at the football.

'Your friend?' said Ugenia.

'He's the only friend I've got!'

'Really?'

'Yes, I'm a castaway – I was in a plane crash and have been stranded here. It's just me and Nelson now.'

'Well, I'm Ugenia Lavender,' said Ugenia. 'How long have you been here?'

'Hmm.' Forrest scratched his

head. 'I'm not sure exactly,' he said, staring at some chalk marks on a tree, 'but I think it's about twenty years.'

'Twenty years! TWENTY YEARS!' cried Ugenia. 'I can't be here twenty years – I have my whole life ahead of me. I have my family and friends, my red bike, Cromer Road.' Ugenia suddenly felt extremely homesick. 'I'll be rescued!' she pronounced.

'That's what I thought,' said Forrest glumly.

'My mum and dad won't forget me! They love me,' cried Ugenia, who then began to sob uncontrollably.

'Er, well, you can hold Nelson for comfort if you like,' said Forrest.

'Er, OK,' whimpered Ugenia, not really knowing how Nelson was going to help.

'I tell you what. I know what will cheer you up. I'll give you a tour of the island!' said Forrest cheerfully. 'Come on, follow me . . .'

And so Forrest, Ugenia and Nelson the football took five steps down the deserted beach.

'OK, so this is the beach, and I sleep over there,' said Forrest, pointing to a shady palm tree.

'And what's that?' asked Ugenia, pointing to the vast jungle terrain.

'Ooh, you must never ever go over there!' said Forrest.

'Why?' asked Ugenia, who was suddenly feeling rather inquisitive.

'Haven't you ever seen the movie *Cannibal Island*?' quivered Forrest.

'Er, no,' replied Ugenia.

'You know, it's the one where the two people go into the jungle and get eaten alive by the natives,' Forrest told her.

'OK, then what about the volcano? Can we go there?'

'But haven't you seen the movie *King Kong*?' Forrest began to shake.

'Er, no,' replied Ugenia.

'You know, it's the one where the big gorilla gets really angry and the cannibals make a sacrifice by giving people to it as presents!'

'OK, then what about the ocean? Do you go swimming?' said Ugenia.

'Haven't you seen the movie *Jaws*?'

Ugenia shook her head.

'You know, the one where the big shark

eats everyone? Or *Splash*, the one with the weirdo mermaid?'

'Er, I think you've been watching way too many movies, they're not real you know!' exclaimed Ugenia, who was beginning to think this Forrest was a bigger scaredy-cat than she was.

'OK, well, you don't have a TV here, Forrest, so what exactly do you do all day?' asked Ugenia.

'Well, I have nice chats with Nelson and I eat these really large coconuts,' replied Forrest.

'Fantastic – can I have some? I'm really hungry!' cried Ugenia.

'Erm, well, I usually wait for them to fall,' said Forrest, nervously pointing at a coconut tree as high as two houses . . .

'INCONVENIENT! I'm hungry now,' moaned Ugenia.

'I have a banana you can have,' offered Forrest.

'You're very kind,' said Ugenia, popping half of it in her mouth and the other half in her luminous yellow rucksack. 'Better make it last!' she explained as she watched a spider monkey swinging from a branch.

Then, suddenly, like a thunderbolt of lightning, Ugenia had a brainwave. 'Inspirational!' she cried. '*I'll* get the coconuts!'

And, before Forrest had time to protest about the dangers, Ugenia, still wearing her luminous yellow rucksack, swiftly began climbing the tree . . . luckily she had her special boots on which had great grip.

Ugenia climbed higher and higher, moving from branch to branch until finally she reached the very top. Slowly she began to reach across to a large, tasty coconut . . . and as she did so she started to lose her balance.

Ugenia felt very scared, her head felt wibbly wobbly. What would Hunk Roberts do right now? she thought. 'Don't look down, don't look down,' breathed Ugenia, trying desperately not to look at the massive drop beneath her as she reached out for the coconut . . .

Ugenia began to sweat. She clung tighter to the trunk of the tree, but the more she told herself not to look down, the more she did . . . she couldn't help it. Suddenly something very weird caught her eye. It was Forrest, who now appeared tiny, standing in a big dug-out sandpit that was almost the shape of a star . . .

'Incredible!' cried Ugenia. 'That almost looks like a footprint!'

Ugenia began waving at Forrest excitedly. 'Look!' Then suddenly the ground began to tremble, the coconut tree began shaking and there was a mighty crack. The branch that Ugenia was clinging to snapped and Ugenia was sent tumbling to ground . . .

'AAAAAAAAAAAAH, I'm going to

die!' she screamed, closing her eyes as she flew through the air before landing with a thud, knocking her head and then passing out. (Thankfully she was saved from any serious damage as she was still wearing her luminous yellow rucksack, which cushioned her fall.)

Ugenia began to stir, as if from a deep sleep, to the beat of bongo drums. As she looked down, she found herself standing between two pillars, her hands bound tightly to each of them, so she couldn't move.

'Wh-where am I!' stammered Ugenia. To her horror she was surrounded by a large crowd of almost naked people with dark charcoal-grey skin, bones through their noses . . . and bits of leaves covering their private bits. They were carrying a

large
cooking pot.
'UUUlli hali hali
hali hali hali,' they chanted.

'Aargh! They're cannibals and they're going to eat me!' cried Ugenia. 'I'm going to die.'

But to add to Ugenia's confusion they marched off, leaving her entirely alone.

Where have they gone? thought Ugenia. 'INJUSTICE! Don't leave me!' she screamed.

Then suddenly Ugenia felt the ground shake, and the two pillars that held her began to tremble.

To Ugenia's horror, she could see something huge in the distance, tearing through the jungle. It was demolishing trees and bounding straight towards her . . .

It was bigger than a house, bigger than a Tyrannosaurus rex, it was ginormous!

It was a GORILLASAURUS REX!

'My dad was right!' Ugenia cried. 'The Gorillasaurus does live on this island, and I'm being sacrificed! The cannibals have left ME! As a present!'

Ugenia could not believe what she was seeing as this massive hairy gorilla loomed over her, beating his chest . . .

'Oo, oo, oooo,' growled the

Gorillasaurus rex.

'No, please . . . no, please! Don't hurt me,' begged Ugenia.

With one mighty swoop, the Gorillasaurus rex swiped Ugenia from the pillars . . . he was that big that she fitted into the palm of his hand . . .

'He's going to crush me! I'm going to die!' screamed Ugenia.

But to Ugenia's surprise, the Gorillasaurus began to gently poke her with his little finger.

'What are you doing?!' snapped Ugenia.

'If you're going to crush me, get on with it! I can't take any more of this!'

The Gorillasaurus then gave Ugenia a very sheepish expression, as if his eyes were trying to say, 'Please be my friend.'

Ugenia smiled back at him. 'I suppose you can be my new New Best Friend. I mean, who knows when I'll see Bronte or Rudy or my mum or dad again,' she sighed, and then she handed her large new NBF the other half of the banana from her luminous yellow rucksack. 'You look even more hungry than me!'

'Aaaaaaah oooh,' grunted the Gorillasaurus.

'Did you just smile?' exclaimed Ugenia, but before the Gorillasaurus had time to answer there was a monumental explosion

. . . It was the volcano! It began to erupt violently and boiling hot molten lava began pouring down the mountain straight towards them.

The Gorillasaurus began running with Ugenia in his arms, cradling her like a baby as he tried to protect her from the boiling hot lava, which began to catch them up rapidly as it surged towards them.

In a flash the lava began to engulf the Gorillasaurus rex. The red hot liquid was up to his nose, he stretched up his arm trying to keep Ugenia safe, and, quickly but gently, placed Ugenia on a hanging branch before finally he was submerged in the sea of red and pulled along by the heavy current.

'No! Don't go! Please don't leave me!' cried Ugenia as she heard the crack of the branch as it began to snap. 'I'm going to die! This is the end.' And Ugenia fell into the red lava, screaming, 'I'M UGENIA LAVENDER, GET ME OUT OF HERE!'

'CUT!' shouted a man with a megaphone from behind a large film camera.

'Hey, kid! You were terrific! Can someone get hair and make-up over here? And we need to do a close-up on the electronic gorilla. This movie is going to be fantastic!'

'Movie?' said Ugenia, who was feeling slightly sick and more than a little bit

44

confused as the hot lava she thought she
was drowning in seemed to feel quite cool
and smelt of sweet tarberry juice. 'And who
are you?' demanded Ugenia to the man
with the megaphone.

'Ah, so you've met my very close friend,
the amazing director Mr Speilbug,' said
Forrest, appearing at her side and helping
Ugenia out of the red gunk.

'But what about this desert island?
You said you were a castaway,' frowned
Ugenia.

'I have been a castaway,' said Forrest. 'I
was preparing for my part.'

'Hey, you're a great little actress,' said
Mr Speilbug. 'Who's your agent? Where
did you come from?'

'Er, er, 13 Cromer Road?' smiled

Ugenia, not really knowing what to say.

'I'm her agent!' said a familiar voice. It was Uncle Harry! And her mum and dad and Granny Betty were behind him.

'Mum, Dad, Uncle Harry, Granny Betty – I'm so glad to see you!' cried Ugenia, throwing her arms around them.

'Thank goodness we found you! I thought you were eating chicken with Uncle Harry,' said Mum.

'And I thought you were fishing with Granny Betty,' said Uncle Harry.

'Yes, thank goodness we've found you!' said Dad. 'We were so worried – you wandered over to the other side of the island! We only managed to find you because we saw your luminous yellow rucksack glowing in the distance.'

'Well, you certainly landed on your feet, love!' chuckled Granny Betty.

'I have saved some roasted chicken and bratwurst for you!' declared Hans the friendly German holidaymaker, coming up behind them.

'Excuse me, Ms Ugenia Lavender,' said Mr Speilbug. 'I was wondering, since you did such a great job, would you consider a starring role in my new movie? We shoot tomorrow! It's a remake called *King Pong Strikes Back 2* – it's a blockbusting, beautiful love story, where two nations are at war yet two hearts fall in love.'

'I'm sorry,' replied Ugenia. 'Right now I have plans to enjoy my holiday with my family – we're in a three-star hotel, meals included. There's entertainment, aqua-aerobics, karaoke, a fish buffet and everything!'

'Well, that's very nice, but we're going to be shooting at the North Pole, Outer Mongolia and the Pacific Ocean. There'll be moose riding, Machu Picchu skiing and hundreds of extras. What da ya think kid?'

'Boring!' smiled Ugenia . . .

Big News!

Hi! Hello!

Wow, now did that top all the adventures I have had so far or what? I mean, come on – gorillas, volcanoes and cannibals . . . I know they were all acting, thank goodness, but even so!

Actually, I felt a bit sad for the

Gorillasaurus rex – even though he was a robot – I kind of felt a connection with the big hairy monkey!

So being in Lamorca with my family was great. I had a fantastic time, and it wasn't boring! And guess what? That Mr Speilbug (or whatever his name was), well, he called up my Uncle Harry (who is my new theatrical agent) and said he's got another movie project he's working on and I might have to go to Hollywood. Never heard of the movie, but it sounds important. He sounded ever so excited, bless him!

Anyway, we'll have to wait and see if that ever happens!

Big XO

Ugenia Lavender XX

Ingenious Top Tip

You don't know what you've got until it's gone

I thought I wasn't going to see my family or you guys again and I realized how important you all are to me.

2

uGenia Lavender

Death Wish

It was a golden morning and the sun was streaming into the kitchen as Ugenia sat with her parents around the table, eating her breakfast.

'I've WON!' shouted Ugenia, leaping into the air and clutching a

green token. 'Well, almost nearly,' she said as she stared at the back of the Wheatie Oatie Flakos' cereal box.

'I need to collect just one more green token and then I've won a free trip to the Lunar Park Funfair as a VIP, which means "Very Important Person"!' exclaimed Ugenia. 'Then I get to go on all the rides as many times as I like without queuing! And I'm allowed to take guests. So, if you're nice to me, I'll take you when I win.'

'Oh, really,' said Ugenia's mother, raising her eyebrows.

'There's this humongous roller coaster,' Ugenia said breathlessly. 'And the scariest ride ever, called the Death Wish, which zooms you upside down and swooshes you through the air really fast . . . it's fantastic!'

'Ooh, I'm not really sure that's my sort of thing,' said Pandora Lavender. 'Perhaps your father will go with you.'

'It sounds ghastly,' said her father. 'Besides, you haven't even won yet.'

'Yeah, but I will win,' said Ugenia. 'I just need to find one more token hidden inside a cereal box, make up a terrific slogan, enter the competition and I'm bound to win.'

Ugenia was utterly convinced she was going to Lunar Park and was already visualizing herself hanging upside down on the Death Wish.

Ugenia spent the first half of the day looking through rubbish bins for another empty box of Wheatie Oatie Flakos, hoping to find that one last token inside the box.

But she had no
luck, so instead
she spent the
second half
of the day
begging her
mother for
some money so she could go and buy some
Wheatie Oatie Flakos instead. Ugenia tried
several different techniques . . .

'I will do the washing-up!'

'Every night this week.'

'I really, really love you. You're the best
mum in the world!'

'If you loved me you would buy them.'

'I hate you . . . you're so mean!'

And then, finally, when Ugenia's best
ideas had dried up, she decided the only

thing left to do was beg . . .

'Pleeeeeeeeeeeeease, pleeeeeeeeeeeeease, pleeeeeeeeeeeeease,' cried Ugenia on her knees, grabbing her mother's leg.

'OK! Enough!' said Pandora Lavender. 'You win, Ugenia! You can have the money, but only if you stop that horrible whinging. It really doesn't suit you and you're giving me a headache,' she complained, handing her two pounds.

'Excellent! Thanks, Mum!' yelled Ugenia, leaping into the air.

'I haven't finished yet,' said Pandora with her hands on her hips. 'There's one condition – whatever cereal you buy you'll have to eat it!'

'Great,' cried Ugenia. 'I wish I could eat Wheatie Oatie Flakos all the time!'

Ugenia jumped on her red bike and pedalled manically towards Rudy's parents' food shop. When Ugenia got to Patels' Food Store, she was hot from pedalling. A rush of excitement swept over her as she thought about finding her green token and winning the VIP trip to Lunar Park – she was one step closer to her queue-jumping dream of dangling upside down on that Death Wish ride.

Ugenia entered the shop to find Mr Patel behind the counter. 'Hi, Mr Patel, do you have any Wheatie Oatie Flakos?' she asked.

'Hmm, let me think,' pondered Mr Patel as his brain tried to recall the last time he had seen a box of that particular cereal. 'Oh, deary, deary me, I think we have sold out.'

'Injustice!' cried Ugenia, suddenly getting rather panicky. I need those Wheatie Oatie Flakos for my Death Wish!'

'Hmm, I see this brand of cereal must be very nutritious,' said Mr Patel. 'Don't fret, Ugenia, no cereal is that special. Hmm, maybe we have some left in the stockroom. Go and join Rudy – he's in there stacking shelves. I'm sure he'll be able to help you find exactly what you're looking for,' added Mr Patel, smiling, as he continued pricing up some large watermelons.

Ugenia ran to the stockroom . . . it was stuffy and dark.

'Ooh, Rudy, you have to help me with my Death Wish. If I don't find a token in the Wheatie Oatie Flakos, I'm doomed

never to get to ride it at the Lunar Park
Funfair.'

'Ah, I was just practising stacking some
up,' smiled Rudy as he proudly presented
a neatly stacked pyramid pile of Wheatie
Oatie Flakos. 'I'm displaying them out on
the shop floor later.'

Ugenia stared in awe at the boxes, which
almost touched the ceiling. 'Ooh, Rudy,

this is magnificent,' she gasped. 'It's just like one of the ancient pyramids in Egypt, where I used to live, stuffed with secret hidden treasure. Except in this case it holds the key to my VIP Death Wish!'

Ugenia carefully took a box of Wheatie Oatie Flakos from the top of the pile. She then ripped open the top, stuck her hand in and fished around for the square green plastic token. But to Ugenia's dismay, all she found inside was Wheatie Oatie Flakos.

'Injustice! I need another,' cried Ugenia, grabbing one more from the top of the pile. Ugenia ripped it open, but there was still no green token. Then she ripped another and another and another. Frantically she was ripping and grabbing and tearing and scratching at the boxes until the large pyramid seemed to disintegrate before their eyes. In fact, it began to wobble and then, as Ugenia took one box too many, it toppled over in a heap. Suddenly, the whole stockroom looked like there had been an explosion of Wheatie Oatie Flakos.

Ugenia and Rudy sat among the mountain of cereal and mass of empty boxes with not one single green Lunar Park Funfair token in sight.

'Uuuuh! Injustice! This is so unfair!' cried Ugenia. 'How on earth am I going get my VIP Death Wish?'

'Well, I think I'm going to get mine,' said Rudy. 'I'm going to be in serious trouble if my parents see this mess . . .'

Ugenia gulped. 'Ooh, Rudy, what have I done? I don't even think I have enough money to pay for it all,' said Ugenia, staring at her two pounds.

'Don't worry about it, let's just get this cleaned up,' said Rudy.

So Rudy and Ugenia began scooping the mountains of Wheatie Oatie Flakos back into the cereal boxes. Ugenia then got some Sellotape and began putting the boxes back up.

'Hopefully no one will notice!' she smiled, trying to make things seem better. Then the pair of them went and stacked the newly packed Wheatie Oatie Flakos in a great pyramid on the shop floor.

'Very nice display! Thank you,' said Mr Patel. 'Ah, Ugenia, did we have what you were looking for?'

'Not quite, Mr Patel, but never mind,'

said Ugenia, quickly pacing out of the shop.

Ugenia gave a look of thanks and remorse to Rudy, as if to say, 'Oops, I'm really sorry. Thanks for being so cool about it. I hope we don't get found out!' and then she jumped on her bike and pedalled 'tokenless' back to 13 Cromer Road.

Ugenia felt very disappointed. Not only had she nearly got Rudy into major trouble. Now she was definitely not going to the Lunar Park Funfair. No green token, no VIP Death Wish.

Ugenia wandered into the kitchen, where her parents were having afternoon tea and toast.

'Ah, Ugenia, did you find the token you wanted?' asked her mother.

'No, I didn't,' said Ugenia sadly,

handing back the two
pounds to her mother.

'Ooh, I'm sorry,'
said her mum.

'But *I* did!'
beamed
her great-
grandmother,
Granny Betty,
walking through the door, proudly holding
a shiny green plastic token. 'Your mum's
just told me you were looking for one. I've
had this for ages!'

'Incredible!' cried Ugenia, punching the
air. 'All I have to do now is fill in the entry
form and enter the competition! I'm going
to be zooming upside down on that Death
Wish before I know it!'

Ugenia ran upstairs and stared at the
entry form, which said: Please give one
sentence telling us why you think you're a
Lunar Park VIP winner . . .

Ugenia began to think of the best answer
she could give. Hmm, well VIP means very
important, so they need to know why I'm
important enough to win? she thought as
she pondered over this and chewed on her
pen before practising her answer on a piece
of paper . . .

I'm a Lunar Park VIP winner
because I'm . . . very nice and lovely.
Nah, too naff . . .

. . . because I'm pretty special.
Although we're all pretty special in
different ways, so my Granny Betty
says. Nah, too fluffy . . .

. . . because I'm going to be really cross and have to kill you if you don't give this to me. Nope, too pushy . . .

I'm a Lunar Park VIP winner because I HAVE WHAT IT TAKES TO RIDE THE DEATH WISH RIDE↓

'Perfect!' said Ugenia as she filled in the application form, put it in an envelope and plopped in all the green tokens she had collected.

Ugenia then got a stamp from her mum and ran to the letter box around the corner, just in time to catch the last post.

One week later, on Saturday morning, Ugenia received a small parcel with a letter

attached. It was from the Wheatie Oatie
Flakos company and said:

Dear Ms Ugenia Lavender . . .
CONGRATULATIONS, YOU'RE A VIP
WINNER!

'I'm a VIP winner!' screamed Ugenia in
excitement, bouncing around the kitchen
like an electric kangaroo who'd had too
much sugar. 'I've won! I'm going to Lunar
Park and I'm going to be zooming upside
down on the Death Wish!'

'That's great, well done, Ugenia,' said
Professor Lavender from behind his large
paper as he sipped his morning coffee.

Ugenia could hardly concentrate as she
began to read the rest of the letter . . .

We are writing to inform you that we loved your entry to be a VIP Lunar Park guest. It was very good, in fact you **almost** won a VIP Lunar Park guest visit, but not quite, as the competition was very fierce . . .

'Injustice!' cried Ugenia, smashing through her father's large newspaper. 'I *almost* won? What does that mean? Who cares about "almost"?!'

Professor Lavender stared blankly at Ugenia. 'Hmm, let me see that letter,' he said, decrumpling his newspaper as Ugenia handed it over. 'Ah, it's not all bad, you've won a consolation prize!'

'What's that?' asked Ugenia.

'Well, it's given to people for their effort when they almost nearly win,'

Professor Lavender explained.

'An almost-nearly prize?' huffed Ugenia as she looked inside the package and pulled out a parcel. Ugenia unwrapped it and untaped the bubble wrap before pulling out . . .

A red plastic purse!

'That's it?' cried Ugenia. 'That's it? All I get is a horrible almost-nearly-winner plastic purse!'

'I think it might come in rather handy,' said Professor Lavender.

But Ugenia wasn't so sure, and spent the rest of the morning feeling rather miffed.

Every time she looked at her red plastic purse she felt even worse.

☆

At midday Ugenia got a phone call from one of her best friends, Crazy Trevor.

'Er, my Uncle Terry has come into town. He works at Lunar Park Funfair. I'm allowed to take my mates . . . he can get us in for free. Do you wanna come?' Crazy Trevor asked.

Ugenia nearly choked on her gooseberry minto with excitement. 'Er, yeah! I would love to!'

'Well, my dad is taking me this evening, so we'll pick you up at five thirty,' said Trevor.

Ugenia ran into the kitchen and dived at her dad, straight into the newly straightened-out newspaper he was reading.

'I'm gonna get to ride my Death Wish!' she shouted. 'I'm gonna ride my Death Wish, Dad. Can I go to Lunar Park tonight, please? It's with Trevor's dad. Please?'

'Only if you let me read my newspaper,' Mr Lavender grunted. 'And if your mum says it's OK.'

Ugenia went hunting for Pandora Lavender. Her mother agreed, but only on the condition that she behaved and stayed close to Trevor's dad the whole time . . .

☆

At 5.30 p.m. Crazy Trevor and his dad, Kevin, pulled up in a large, rusty white van outside 13 Cromer Road. Ugenia was all ready to go. Pandora Lavender followed her out into the street, chatted with Kevin about details like safety and what time they would be back home, then handed Ugenia the red plastic purse. 'There's some money in there just in case,' she said.

'Thanks, Mum,' said Ugenia, half grateful for the money but equally horrified

75

at the nasty looking red plastic almost-
nearly-winner purse. Ugenia shoved it in
the back pocket of her jeans and climbed
into the back seat, where Rudy and Bronte
were already sitting.

Kevin started the engine and the white
van clunked down Boxmore Hill, past the
twenty-four-hour, bargain-budget, bulk-
buyers' supersized supermarket and into the
town centre . . .

Then they headed to the edge of town
towards the wasteland, where the lights
of Lunar Park twinkled in the distance.
Ugenia could hardly wait as they drove
along the vast long road that swept up to
the entrance of the funfair. She could hear
the terrorized screams – her Death Wish
dream was getting closer.

Crazy Trevor and his dad, Ugenia, Rudy and Bronte piled out into the dusty car park, where the large neon Lunar Park sign was glowing above them.

'Once we're through those gates, everything is free!' said Rudy. 'And we get to go on everything!'

'This is so kind of your uncle to sort us out tickets,' said Bronte.

'And I finally get to go on my Death Wish!' said Ugenia excitedly.

'Follow me!' said Kevin, who started to walk in the opposite direction to the ticket entrance.

Ugenia, Bronte, Rudy and Crazy Trevor followed Kevin round to the side of the wire fence. It was a little bit dark and there were lots of caravans and electric dynamos whirling.

'Where on earth are we going?' asked Bronte, who was feeling a little bit uneasy.

'We're taking the cheeky VIP entrance, care of my bruvva,' said Kevin. 'He can get us in for nuffin'.'

'But I thought your brother worked here?

Surely he can get us proper tickets?' said Bronte.

'Ah, well, he doesn't actually work here,' said Kevin. 'He's just been hired to fix a generator for the bumper cars.'

Suddenly, out of the darkness, Uncle Terry appeared from behind a caravan inside the fence. 'All right, kids, come on in . . . ready for some funfair action!' he said as he began pulling the wire fence away from the ground.

Kevin got on his hands and knees and wiggled on his round belly under the fence.

'This is ingenious!' said Ugenia.

'This is dishonest,' said Bronte.

'This is cheaper,' said Rudy.

Ugenia, suddenly feeling like her favourite action hero, Hunk Roberts, dived

and rolled under the fence.

'Come on, Bronte. Don't be a scaredy-cat, I dare you!' said Ugenia from the other side of the fence.

'Oh, very well,' gulped Bronte as she followed everyone else and crawled under.

Once they were all finally through and everyone had straightened themselves out, Ugenia, Bronte, Rudy and Crazy Trevor followed Kevin and Terry into a white tent.

'Now, me and Kevin are going to have a nice can of something,' said Terry. 'So that means you can all go off and enjoy yourselves. Remember you can go on anything you like.'

'What, by ourselves? Without an adult?' said Bronte.

'Yeah, you'll be fine, just keep together. Don't get up to any mischief, cos we'll be right here keeping a close eye on you,' said Terry, who was waving a five-pound note, trying to get the barman's attention.

'Great!' said Ugenia.

'Fabulous,' said Rudy.

'Er . . . yeah,' said Crazy Trevor.

'Let's be real daredevils and find my Death Wish!' said Ugenia.

And so Ugenia, Crazy Trevor, Rudy and Bronte quickly walked out of the tent before Kevin and Terry could change their minds.

Directly in front of them was a black
tent that had an old swirly sign saying:
MYSTICAL MYSTERIES . . .

Crazy Trevor, Ugenia, Rudy and Bronte
stared at the sign. They were just about to
go in when Trevor said, 'I'm not going in
there – it looks boring, thanks very much.'

'Come on, Trevor – now you can't be
a scaredy-cat, I dare you!' said Ugenia,
dragging Trevor into the tent before he had
any time to argue.

Ugenia, Trevor, Bronte and Rudy were
welcomed by a man who was wearing just
a pair of underpants. He had a bald head
and his body was completely blue all over
with jigsaw-puzzle-shaped tattoos.

'Hello, I am the Blue Enigma,' said the
blue man, ushering Ugenia, Rudy, Crazy

Trevor and Bronte inside the tent.

'Why are you blue?' asked Ugenia.

'Ah, that's the enigma – I'm a mystery,' he said.

'Yes, you certainly are a bit different,' smiled Ugenia politely, desperately trying not to stare at his underpants.

'Er . . . yeah,' said Trevor.

'Now, ladies and gentlemen,' the Blue Enigma started. 'Are you ready to meet Mystical Marge? Do you have enough courage to look into your futures? Go through into the back room, but trust me it's not for the faint-hearted.'

Ugenia looked at the red velvet curtains that the Blue Enigma was pointing to. 'Come on, let's go on in there!' she said.

'Nah, I'm not that bovvered about my future, thanks very much,' said Trevor.

'Yes, my dad says we should just trust and live for the day!' said Rudy.

'And I'd rather not know, thanks,' said Bronte.

'Ah, you bunch of chickens!' said Ugenia, who then marched through the red curtains without them.

The back room had dark red lined walls and was dimly lit by tiny little red lamps. There was a lady with a large crystal ball sitting at a table.

'Aha, come in, come in. I've been expecting you!' said Mystical Marge, who was wearing a black headscarf and big dangly earrings.

'Really?' said Ugenia as she walked over to the table suspiciously.

'Yes, and something red and nasty is following you,' said Mystical Marge.

'OK, thanks a lot,' said Ugenia politely, thinking this lady seemed quite batty, when suddenly she noticed a short figure standing in the corner hiding in the shadows.

Ugenia could barely see the little man's face as it was masked by a red hooded

85

cloak, but he had a large nose that was poking out and he was breathing very heavily.

Ugenia took a slow step forward. Suddenly the red dwarfed figure glared at her, as if he could read every single thing she was thinking. He then made a hissing sound like a spiteful cat that had seen its worst enemy. Ugenia jumped back with fright.

'Beware of your death wish,' whispered Mystical Marge to Ugenia.

What a load of rubbish, thought Ugenia as she quickly backed out of the room to where Bronte, Rudy and Crazy Trevor were waiting. 'Let's forget about all this, I wanna go on my Death Wish ride,' she said, feeling rather uneasy as she tried to forget the creepy dwarf and what Mystical Marge had said.

Ugenia's friends quickly followed her outside and into the summer evening breeze.

Ugenia instantly felt better as the smell of candyfloss and hot dogs wafted under her nose . . .

'Come on, let's get some supplies!' said Trevor with excitement, running up to a large van that had ice creams, meat pies and fizzy cherryade.

'I'd like a chocolate milkshake and a large raspberry ripple with a flake in, please, with extra sprinkles of nuts and hundreds and thousands,' said Crazy Trevor. 'Oh, and some cherry fudge sauce. Yeah, and don't hold back with that.'

'I'll have a hot dog,' said Ugenia, just about to reach for her red plastic purse in her back pocket, when she suddenly remembered that everything was free in Lunar Park.

Rudy and Bronte shared a candyfloss.

And they all walked happily towards their next target, the T. REX TWISTER . . .

The T. Rex Twister ride consisted of small green pods, each with four seats in them, that were whizzing in and out of a large Tyrannosaurus rex's mouth, which was snapping ferociously.

'That looks fantastic!' said Ugenia, running towards the gate for the next pod. 'Come on, let's go on it!'

'I can't, I'm busy eating!' said Trevor.

'I dare you, come on and eat at the same

time . . .' said Ugenia. 'It's stopping. Let's get on it!'

'Er, I'm not sure about this,' said Trevor, climbing into the pod with his raspberry ripple and chocolate milkshake.

'Erm, I'm not so sure about this either,' squirmed Bronte, staring at the large teeth. 'It looks like it might be dangerous . . .'

'Don't worry, it's electric, it won't really eat you!' laughed Ugenia, dragging Bronte towards a green pod.

And before Bronte had any time to protest, she and Ugenia, along with Trevor and Rudy, were held in with an iron bar across their laps.

The pods whipped and jerked back and forth as they narrowly missed the sharp dino gnashers that snapped at them.

Bronte and Ugenia screamed and giggled. 'This is fantastic!' squealed Bronte as the pod jerked sideways, squashing her into Ugenia, who lunged into Rudy, who then lunged at Crazy Trevor, who was still trying to eat his raspberry ripple and sip his chocolate milkshake without spilling it.

The chocolate milkshake flew over their heads on to the pod behind them, straight into a man's face, just as his pod was flung forwards and whizzed out of the dinosaur's bottom, which made a large farting sound.

'Perfect timing!' laughed Crazy Trevor as the music slowed down and the ride came to a halt.

After the ride was over and their heads had stopped spinning, Ugenia and her friends staggered over to the Evolution Log Ride – it was a roller coaster that sped through a river and soaked everyone with water.

Rudy sat at the front. Ugenia sat behind him, then Bronte, then Trevor.

'Why do I have to sit in the front?' said Rudy.

'It means you're a VIP – a very important person,' said Ugenia, smiling.

'Erm, I not sure about this,' said Rudy,

who was trying to get Trevor's raspberry
ripple out of his jeans. 'I really don't want
to get my hair wet.'

'Don't worry, you'll be fine!' said Ugenia.

And before Rudy had any time to
protest, they were zooming down the steep
waterfall on a huge log.

They all screamed with laughter as they reached the bottom and a humongous wave drenched Rudy at the front.

'I'm not impressed. I'll get you back,' he grumbled, trying not to smile.

'Ah, it means you're an extra-special VIP the more wet you get,' said Ugenia as she ran them over to the Midsummer Night Scream Phantom Ghost Train.

Bronte and Trevor got in a separate car in front of them. But just as Ugenia was about to get on board with Rudy, she noticed a flash of red cloak among the crowds of people coming towards the train. Was that the creepy dwarf? Nah, it must be my imagination, thought Ugenia as she got into the small car with Rudy, who was trembling slightly.

'Ooh, Ugenia, I'm not so sure about this. It looks a little bit scary,' said Rudy as they watched Bronte and Trevor disappear through the black doors into the dark tunnel ahead of them.

'Don't worry, come on . . . you've got to be a daredevil!' said Ugenia. 'Besides, you're not alone. I'm with you!'

Their car began to glide on its rails

towards the large black doors. They were just about to enter the tunnel when something made Ugenia turn round.

The red dwarf was climbing into the carriage behind them, giving Ugenia a nasty glare.

'Something red and nasty *is* following me!' cried Ugenia. 'Mystical Marge was right.'

'What on earth are you talking about?' said Rudy, who was gripping Ugenia.

'I don't know exactly, but that red dwarf behind us is nasty,' said Ugenia.

Ugenia and Rudy rolled into the blackness to the sound of wails and screams. They approached a headless body followed by a wailing ghoul.

Ugenia could hear the car behind them

with the red dwarf in it. She stared at the body that had lost its head then suddenly, like a thunderbolt of lightning, Ugenia had a brainwave . . .

'Ingenious! We must lose the dwarf!'

With no time to lose, Ugenia jumped out of the car, dragging Rudy with her. They leaped over the tracks, down the side of the tunnel and into the darkness.

One minute later, the red dwarf chugged past in his car. Ugenia held her breath as she and Rudy hid behind a large glowing cauldron.

'Phew, he didn't see us, Rudy,' whispered Ugenia.

Rudy and Ugenia stood very still. It was very dark and quiet . . . no other cars came through.

Then, out of the shadows, a dark figure came towards them. Rudy began to tremble, so did Ugenia. 'It's the red dwarf . . . he's coming to get us!'

But suddenly a tall man in a black T-shirt and jeans shone a flashlight at them.

'What are you doing getting out of a car?' he yelled. 'That's not allowed!' He grabbed Rudy and Ugenia by the arm and escorted them both straight out of the tunnel and back into the bright lights of the fairground.

Bronte and Trevor were waiting for them, smiling.

'What happened to you?' asked Bronte. 'Your car came out empty!'

'We had a nasty red dwarf following us,' said Ugenia.

'Hmm, well he's not here now,' said Bronte.

'Come on then, Ugenia,' said Crazy Trevor. 'I reckon it's time to go on your Death Wish.' He grinned.

So they climbed down from the ghost train, turned the corner and manoeuvred through the crowds till there in front of them was the gigantic, humongous Death Wish.

It was a yellow and black metal crane, which was twice as tall as the Dinosaur Museum where Ugenia's dad worked. The whole ride had only four seats with seriously high backs – like they were going to be launched into space.

Ugenia stared at the iron monstrosity and began to feel a little bit nervous. It looked so big and high. 'Erm, I'm not so sure,' she said.

'Come on, you're the daredevil,' said Crazy Trevor. 'Let's go!'

'Erm, you go first,' squirmed Ugenia, who began to think about Mystical Marge's Death Wish warning.

'Ah, you're not being a chicken, are you?' said Rudy 'After what you've dragged me through?'

'Ugenia, you're the brave one!' said Bronte.

Ugenia hesitated, but before she had any time to protest, she found herself following her three best friends on to the launch pad.

Ugenia and Rudy sat on the two black chairs on one side, and Crazy Trevor and Bronte sat on the other two. A serious-looking man came over and belted them all in, then he pulled down a very heavy

contraption which locked them in tightly so they couldn't move a muscle.

The Death Wish gave a hiss and began to slowly pull back the chairs, elevating them higher and higher, preparing for the pendulum to take its first swing.

Ugenia was so high in the sky she felt like she could lick the stars. As she looked down at her feet, which wiggled above the tiny fair below, she felt a tidal wave of fear sweep over her. Ugenia held her breath and began to sweat as the chair rotated and she was now dangling upside down. Suddenly Ugenia could see the whole world from another point of view. She began to regret how much she had wanted to go on the Death Wish ride. She wished she had never laid eyes on that stupid breakfast cereal Wheatie Oatie Flakos.

Ugenia's heart began to beat faster and faster in anticipation as she waited for the metal crane's pendulum to take its first swing, then suddenly she noticed a flash of red down by the controls below. It was the red dwarf, glaring up at Ugenia.

'It's the nasty red dwarf,' Ugenia hissed. 'He's come to get me! Beware of the Death Wish – that's what Mystical Marge said! I want to get off!' Ugenia shouted, not feeling like such a daredevil after all.

But before Ugenia had any more time to panic, the Death Wish creaked and pulled back a final couple of centimetres and then suddenly released and zoomed Ugenia upside down through the air.

'I'm going to die!' screamed Ugenia.

'This is fabulous,' cried Rudy.

'I hate this Death Wish!' shrieked Ugenia.

'I love it,' said Bronte.

Ugenia closed her eyes. It felt like she was going a million miles an hour as she sped through the night sky, heading down towards the floor. Her face began to flatten in the wind and her head felt like it would explode as the crane then swung all the way to the other side like a speeding pendulum clock. It then jolted and repeated the same motion backwards.

Ugenia began to feel faint as all the blood rushed to her face. She wished this horrendous experience could be over. The Death Wish took its final bow and they were returned to the launch pad.

Ugenia sighed as the heavy metal contraption released and she jumped out of her seat, feeling a rush of relief, excitement and horror all at once.

'He was trying to kill me – he was fiddling with the controls!' cried Ugenia, pointing at the red dwarf.

Crazy Trevor, Rudy, and Bronte huddled around Ugenia as the glaring red dwarf approached the launch pad and walked towards Ugenia.

'You stay away from me,' Ugenia cried. 'Mystical Marge warned me about you! You're the something red and nasty that's following me!'

The dwarf's expression broke out into a smile as he reached into his pocket. 'Ah, she was right!' said the dwarf. 'I was following you – to hand you back the plastic purse you dropped in the tent. It is red and a bit nasty, but it's got money in it.'

Ugenia stared at the dwarf, dumbfounded.

'I thought *you* were nasty,' said Ugenia, feeling a bit embarrassed. 'You hissed at me earlier.'

'I was just clearing my throat,' laughed the dwarf. 'It's the fairground dust – being so short it goes up my nose!'

'Oh! Ah! Well then, that explains it. It's

very kind of you to return my horrid purse! Thank you,' Ugenia said gratefully and, with a wave of relief, she took back her almost-nearly-winner red plastic purse.

Ugenia, Crazy Trevor, Rudy and Bronte said their goodbyes to the not-so-nasty red dwarf and decided it was time to go back to Kevin and Terry at the tent.

'Get up to much mischief?' said Kevin as they pushed back the entrance flap.

'Us?' said Trevor. 'Course not. We just went on the teacup ride.'

Ugenia, Crazy Trevor, Bronte, Rudy and Kevin then walked out of the front entrance of Lunar Park, got back in the rusty white van and happily went home.

The next day there was a knock at Ugenia's front door. It was Rudy's father, Ranjid Patel, with a large cardboard parcel.

'Hello, Ranjid,' said Ugenia's mum.

'Hello, Pandora. I have a message from Rudy for Ugenia to say thank you for his VIP soaking on the Evolution Log Ride at Lunar Park,' he said, handing over a large cardboard parcel.

Ugenia opened it and stared at twenty boxes of Wheatie Oatie Flakos taped up with Sellotape . . .

'Hmm, my favourite, thanks, Mr Patel,' smiled Ugenia politely.

Big News!

Hello, hello . . .

So this isn't one of my news updates based on good behaviour!

Sometimes I gotta let my hair down and turn the world upside down, and actually I then get to see things clearly. I'm not such a daredevil all the time and little red dwarfs are quite kind once you get to know them!

Yeah, maybe I didn't get the VIP treatment I was hoping for, but it was such a laugh anyway. Being with my mates is what matters . . . and actually they turned out braver than I did in the end.

And as for Rudy – he certainly got me back for that soaking with all those Wheatie Oatie Flakos! His dad basically found out what I'd done. He was a bit cross, but said I could have them anyway. And I've been helping Rudy stack some shelves to say sorry. The whole of the Lavender family is now living on Wheatie Oatie Flakos.

Oh, it's all part of a day's work for me. Ugenia Lavender over and out!

Big XO
Ugenia Lavender XX

Ingenious Top Tip

Careful what you wish for...

I got my death wish and hated it, and I got my wish to eat Wheatie Oatie Flakos all the time and I'm sick of them!

3

uGenia Lavender

Home Alone

Ugenia woke up on Friday morning to the sound of her mother, Pandora, yelling up the stairs.

'Ugenia Lavender! Hurry up! I'm going to be late for work!'

'All right, all right, I'm coming!' yelled Ugenia, leaping out of bed and dashing to the bathroom. She threw on her clothes and manically packed her luminous yellow rucksack.

113

Ugenia's mum was giving Ugenia a lift
to school and taking her dad, Professor
Edward Lavender, to the Dinosaur
Museum. Pandora was doing a new
entertainment slot at nine o'clock, which
meant she only had forty-five minutes to
drop them off and get to the studio on time,
and she wanted to make a good impression.

'Hurry, Ugenia, I can't be late,' called
Pandora, busy polishing her most precious
porcelain ancient-
tribal-statue
headpiece. 'It's
live TV and
I have a new
boss, so I need
everything to
go smoothly.

And tidy your room – it's a pigsty!'

'All right, all right!' groaned Ugenia. She ran into the dining room and quickly grabbed her science project from the table, which made Pandora's most precious porcelain ancient-tribal-statue headpiece wobble.

'Ugenia, be careful, for goodness sake, try to be a bit more responsible!' shrieked Pandora. 'That was a special present from your father from his trip to Kathmandu.'

Ugenia rushed out of the front door to find her dad already sitting calmly in the front seat of their beige Mini. She squeezed herself in the back and then fastened her seat belt. Pandora, who was wearing her brand-new cream suit, dashed to the car and started the engine.

'I've forgotten my salad-cream sandwiches! One second,' said Edward Lavender, hopping out of the car and running into the house.

'EEEEdwaaard! I'm going to be late,' screeched Pandora.

'Calm down, woman, it won't take a minute,' said Professor Lavender.

Three very long minutes later, Edward was back in the Mini and the Lavenders were on their way to take Ugenia to school.

But as they pulled out of Cromer Road, there were huge roadworks causing heavy traffic.

'I'm going to be late!' shrieked Pandora as the Mini crawled along like a miserable snail, stuck between a monstrous dustbin lorry and a twenty-four-hour, bargain-budget, bulk-buyers' supersized-supermarket large lorry.

Pandora huffed in frustration. Ugenia giggled at her mum.

'Ugenia, it's not easy being me,' snapped Pandora. 'Just you wait until you're a grown-up with lots of responsibilities.'

'Yeah, yeah, I can't wait,' groaned Ugenia.

Ugenia decided the best thing to do was to embrace the delay and have light refreshments with a flask of tarberry juice.

'Glass anyone?' said Ugenia, offering her mother a plastic cup just as Pandora gave an almighty sneeze, sending the tarberry juice flying all over her beautiful cream suit.

'For goodness sake!' wailed Pandora. 'Look what you've done, you silly girl.'

'But it was an accident!' cried Ugenia. 'I was only trying to be helpful.'

'Edward, do something!' shouted Pandora as she tried to wipe herself down and drive at the same time.

'Just pay attention to the road!' grunted Edward.

'Don't tell me what to do, it's all your fault – if you hadn't made us late!' snapped Pandora.

'Well, maybe we should have left earlier!' barked Edward.

'Well, maybe if I didn't have so much to do!' griped Pandora.

'Well, maybe you should both stop arguing!' shouted Ugenia, just as the gigantic dustbin lorry in front of them squealed to a halt.

Quickly Pandora slammed on her brakes. The car skidded forward and was followed by a loud crunch as the supermarket lorry slammed into them.

Frantically Pandora tried to control
the spinning steering wheel as their Mini
hurtled forward and flew straight into
the back of the dustbin lorry, which had
just been filled with all the Cromer Road
weekly rubbish.

'Aaaaaaah,' yelled Pandora as she was
flung forward and headbutted the steering
wheel.

'Aaaaaaooooooooooh!' screamed
Professor Lavender as he bumped his nose
on the dashboard.

'Ugenia, are you OK? Ugenia?' said
Mum and Dad in unison. But before
Ugenia had time to answer, mountains
of stinky, pongy rubbish spilt on to the
Mini. Pandora, Edward and Ugenia
screamed in horror as they were engulfed

with mouldy carrots and cabbage.

Suddenly Ugenia's ears were drowned with the sound of sirens, and an ambulance, a fire engine and a police car swiftly arrived on the scene.

'Don't move a muscle,' said a paramedic.

'I'll get you out,' said a fireman.

'Can I see your licence?' said a policeman.

Speedily a fireman in a yellow rubber suit began cutting the Mini, which now looked like a very squashed prawn mayonnaise sandwich, in half to release the Lavenders.

Edward, Pandora and Ugenia were lifted on to stretchers and carried into the back of a gleaming white ambulance which sparkled with importance. The paramedics began examining the Lavenders and talking very complicated words into their walkie-talkie radios.

'Have a doctor on standby,' said one paramedic.

Ne-Nah, Ne-Nah, Wooo woo-oh wooh, whirled the ambulance, as if to say, 'Get

out of the way, you idiots, we have an emergency!'

The ambulance sped the Lavenders down Boxmore Hill, past the twenty-four-hour, bargain-budget, bulk-buyers' supersized supermarket into the town centre, past the Dinosaur Museum and straight to the general hospital's Accident and Emergency Department.

A few minutes later, the Lavenders were lying on trolleys and whizzing down the hospital corridors into an examination room. Three pristine white beds and a very handsome doctor were waiting for them. It was Doctor Clooney, who had been at the same college as Pandora when she was a student.

'Hello, Pandora,' said Doctor Clooney,

beginning to examine her gently. 'Well, it looks as though you could have a broken nose, a splintered shoulder and a possible fractured arm.'

'Is that serious?' whimpered Pandora, trying to be brave.

'Yes, moderately serious. I need to get you X-rayed to check,' said Doctor Clooney.

'OK,' said Pandora obediently.

Doctor Clooney then gave Professor Edward Lavender a prod and a poke.

'Ouch,' yelled Professor Lavender.

'Well, it looks like you could have a fractured jaw, a broken rib, a broken wrist, a broken leg and a minor fracture to your skull with concussion,' announced Doctor Clooney.

'Really?' said the Professor. 'Is that serious?'

'Yes, very serious, so I'm sending you straight into surgery.'

'Er, excuse me! What about me? Shouldn't I have gone first?' interrupted Ugenia as her parents were wheeled off down the corridor. 'I'm the child here – they're the grown-ups.' She huffed, feeling a bit left out of all the attention that her parents were getting.

'Ah, little lady! The paramedics warned me what was wrong with you,' said Doctor Clooney. 'That's why I left the best till last. Let's have a look at you.' And very smoothly and efficiently, Doctor Clooney began to examine Ugenia. 'Just as I thought,' he said finally.

'What's wrong with me? Will I live? Is it serious?' squirmed Ugenia, who began thrashing around on her bed.

'No, not exactly,' laughed Doctor Clooney, 'unless you consider a bruised little finger life-threatening!'

'INJUSTICE! Is that it?' huffed Ugenia, who was very disappointed with her diagnosis. 'That's so unfair. Why is it the grown-ups always get the good stuff?'

'What do you mean? You're a very

lucky young lady!' frowned Doctor
Clooney, applying a plaster to her little
finger. Now, let's see how your parents are
doing.'

And so Ugenia followed Doctor Clooney
down a corridor and into the main hospital
to find her mum and dad. There they were,
in a ward, wrapped in casts and bandages,
looking extremely bruised and miserable.
They both lay on their beds and groaned.

'Ooh, I feel awful,' whimpered Pandora.

'Ooh, I feel terrible,' moaned Edward.

'Well, it looks like we shall have to keep
you both in under observation,' said Doctor
Clooney. 'You will need plenty of rest and
relaxation without any worrying.'

'Ugenia, we've just phoned Uncle Harry
and he has offered to take care of you

until we get home,' smiled Dad through his bandages. 'He'll be there when you get back.'

'And my old friend Doctor Clooney has kindly offered to take you back to Cromer Road,' said Pandora. 'You will be OK, won't you?' she finished, passing Ugenia the front doorkey.

'Sure, I'll be fine,' smiled Ugenia, thinking that at last this was her chance to be a grown-up.

'Are you sure?' said her mum anxiously.

'Mum, I'll be totally cool, don't worry! Trust me, I'm nine! I can look after myself!' announced Ugenia.

'Well, tell Uncle Harry that there's money in the kitchen drawer and to ring me on my mobile if there are any problems,' said her mum.

And so Doctor Clooney drove Ugenia past the twenty-four-hour, bargain-budget, bulk-buyers' supersized supermarket and up Boxmore Hill until finally they stopped outside 13 Cromer Road.

'Now, Ugenia Lavender, your parents need to rest without any stress, so please be on your best behaviour for Uncle Harry,' said Doctor Clooney. 'You need to be a grown up young lady.'

'Yeah, all right! My Uncle Harry will take care of me anyway,' huffed Ugenia as she slammed the car door and put her new grown-up house key in the lock. 'That Clooney needs to get out more,' she muttered to herself.

Ugenia stepped inside the house, it felt

cold and empty. 'Uncle Harry, I'm back!'
There was no reply – only silence. That's
weird – Mum and Dad said he would be
here, she thought.

Ugenia noticed the answering machine
was flashing. She pressed the button.

'Hi, Edward and Pandora, Harry here.
I couldn't hear every word you said on the
phone – the kitchen was so noisy. I can
definitely look after Ugenia *next week* – I
think that's what you said. Call
me on my mobile as
I'm off to the
USA for a
couple of days.
Beep . . . you
have no more
messages,'

said the answering machine.

Ugenia froze. Uncle Harry had obviously misunderstood the arrangements. What did it all mean?

Suddenly it hit her – Ugenia Lavender was HOME ALONE!

'Hmm, maybe I should call my parents,' thought Ugenia aloud. 'But Doctor Clooney did say I should be a grown-up and they do need a rest.'

Then, suddenly, like a thunderbolt of lightning, Ugenia had a brainwave. 'Ingenious!' she cried. 'I'm in charge! I can be a grown-up – how hard can that be?'

Ugenia decided that she should act like it was any normal weekday afternoon for any normal responsible grown-up.

'I'll prepare tonight's dinner!' she said

to herself. Proudly she peered inside the
fridge. It was empty except for one lonely
pickled gherkin and half a can of sardines
that looked like they had been up all night
fighting.

She looked in the cupboards to find only
twenty-five cans of baked beans and a
piece of garlic.

'Beans! I can't live on just beans. What
would a grown-up do?'

Then, suddenly, like a thunderbolt
of lightning, Ugenia had a brainwave.
Incredible! thought Ugenia. Food shopping!
I'll go to the supermarket.

Ugenia grabbed fifteen pounds from the
kitchen drawer and jumped on her red bike,
feeling really grown up as she sped down
Boxmore Hill. 'Yeah, I can do this, being a

grown-up isn't so hard, right?'

Ugenia parked her bike, grabbed a large trolley and wandered into the ginormous twenty-four-hour, bargain-budget, bulk-buyers' supersized supermarket. She stared at the tall shelves, stuffed with biscuits, beetroot, bubble bath, pasta, prawns, parsnips, tomatoes, turnips, turkey, salami, shampoo, smoked salmon and a mountain of washing powder that was stacked as high as a skyscraper looming over her.

Ugenia felt slightly confused by so much selection. She stared at the very efficient people with their shopping lists.

'Rats! I should have made a list too. Still, I'll just have to make do,' she declared as she began loading her trolley with bread rolls, ham, pineapple, popcorn, parsnips, olives, ice cream, macaroons and finally a large family sized packet of toilet rolls.

'Ah, broccoli, grown-ups always eat broccoli.'

'Ah, washing-up liquid, grown-ups always do the washing-up.'

'Ah, salmon, grown-ups always eat salmon,' announced Ugenia as she approached the cashier, feeling rather pleased with herself for her grown-up choices.

134

The shop assistant at the till was wearing a blue nylon uniform, a name badge that said 'Angela' and a very bored expression.

Angela rang up Ugenia's items. 'That's twenty pounds, please.'

Ugenia stared in her purse. She had only fifteen. 'I don't have enough money,' said Ugenia, who suddenly felt a bit embarrassed.

'Well, you'll just have to put some things back then, won't you,' said Angela blankly.

Ugenia stared at her pile of shopping and tried to decide what should go.

'Oh, hurry up,' sighed the man in the queue behind her.

'We haven't got all day,' said the woman behind him.

'Come on, love,' huffed another lady

behind her as the queue began to grow.

Ugenia began to feel slightly panicky. 'Er, the toilet roll? No, I need that. The salmon? No. Broccoli? No. The popcorn? No, I definitely need the popcorn!'

Meanwhile, the large queue behind began to give more impatient sighs. Just as Ugenia was about to freak out and make a run for it, she heard a familiar voice.

'Hello! Ugenia! It's me, Colleen.'

'Hello there,' said Ugenia, who was a bit confused. What was Colleen doing back from Lamorca? And what was she doing in a twenty-four-hour, bargain-budget, bulk-buyers' supersized supermarket blue nylon uniform?

'I couldn't handle being a rep in Lamorca any longer,' said Colleen. 'All that karaoke and aqua-aerobics. I've gone up in the world now – I'm the Assistant Deputy Consulting Produce and Livestock Floor Supervisor!' smiled Colleen. 'Since you and your family were so lovely to me out in Lamorca I want to help you out with your shopping. Angela, give her my staff discount – that should cover the difference.'

'Wow, thank you!' said Ugenia gratefully.

Ugenia then proudly wheeled out her ten bags of shopping into the car park. How am I supposed to get all this home? she thought as she stared at the trolley, then at her bike. This was proving more difficult than she thought.

Suddenly, like a thunderbolt of lightning, Ugenia had a brainwave. 'Invention!' she cried. 'A trolley-pulling bike!'

Ugenia just so happened to have a thick piece of rope in her luminous yellow rucksack (it was one of those just-in-case-of-emergency things and this was it!). She tied the trolley to her bike and slowly cycled

up Boxmore Hill.

'This is proving to be harder than I thought,' puffed Ugenia.

But finally, Ugenia reached 13 Cromer Road and thought about what a grown-up would do next.

'Make a cup of tea, put the shopping away and then plan supper!' exclaimed Ugenia.

So Ugenia put the kettle on, stuffed the fridge with all ten bags of shopping, including the toilet rolls and shampoo, then squeezed the door shut with a big sigh of relief.

Ugenia listened to the lonely sound of
the electrical groan of the fridge. The house
felt very cold and empty suddenly, when
she remembered she was home alone, all
by herself.

'I'm OK, I'm practically grown up,' said
Ugenia, trying to make herself feel better.
What do grown-ups do at dinner time
anyway?'

Ugenia stared at the dining-room table.
It had a pretty, lacy tablecloth with delicate
china dinner plates on it, and in
the very middle was her mother's most
precious porcelain ancient-tribal-statue
headpiece.

Suddenly, like a thunderbolt of lightning,
Ugenia had a brainwave, 'Invitations! I'll
have a dinner party!' she cried.

Ugenia quickly rang her best friend. 'Rudy, I have a plan,' said Ugenia in her best, grown-up voice. 'It's a bit of a tricky mission impossible called "Dining with Ms Lavender". I'll need the best people for the job, dedication and loyalty, so call Trevor and Bronte for help right away. Meet immediately round at mine.'

Rudy quickly made a couple of calls and rushed over to Ugenia's. Bronte and Trevor came round a few minutes later.

'As your dinner-party planner, I thought we need to focus on four major points,' announced Rudy, pulling down his latest vision board, which had 'Rudy's Mission Impossible Plans' on it in big black marker pen.

DINING WITH MS LAVENDER:

1. MENU - UGENIA. MUST BE SCRUMPTIOUS AND TASTY.

2. TABLE SETTING - BRONTE. DELICATE, SIMPLE STYLE NEEDED, WITH APPROPRIATE CUTLERY.

3. GUEST LIST - TREVOR. WHO WE INVITE IS VITAL - THEY MUST BE INTERESTING, STIMULATING AND CURRENTLY COOL (RUDY TO APPROVE).

4. DINNER IS SERVED AT A CIVILIZED TIME - 7 P.M. PROMPT.

'Very nice,' said Bronte.

'Love it,' said Ugenia.

'Er . . . yeah,' said Trevor.

'Now remember,' said Rudy, 'this is a fine, elegant, stylish dinner party. There will be good conversation, light chit-chat and plenty of small talk! Here is a list of guests

for you to invite.' Rudy
handed Trevor a list of names:

SITA
MAX
CARA
BILLY
SEBASTIAN
CHANTELLE
LIBERTY
ANOUSHKA
LARA

* RUDY'S *
MISSION
IMPOSSIBLE
PLANS!

'Actually, I have a question,' said Bronte.
'Where're your mum and dad?'

Ugenia gulped.

'Er, they have just popped out for a bit.
They needed some time to themselves,'

said Ugenia, determined to manage this situation by herself and be a grown-up. 'Anyway, our dinner guests will be here in one hour, we have work to do!'

And so Bronte laid the table, Ugenia went to the kitchen to make mountains of food – with Rudy's guidance – and Trevor began calling everyone.

'Sounds great.'

'Yes, I can come.'

'I'll bring a friend.'

'A party! With food!'

'Yeah, I'll bring my mates.'

'Oh, yeah, can I bring my brothers?'

'Er . . . yeah, OK,' said Trevor.

Before they knew it, everything was ready. The table looked immaculate, there was a

magnificent
spread of
food with
humongous
plates of
parsnips,
pineapples,
popcorn,

macaroons, olives, ham, ice cream and
bread rolls. And for napkins there was a
family sized packet of toilet rolls.

'Excellent!' said Rudy.

'Very nice,' said Bronte.

'Love it,' said Ugenia.

'Yeah,' said Trevor.

Suddenly it was seven o'clock and the
doorbell rang. An avalanche of people
came pouring in.

Sita, who had brought her friend Sandra, who had brought Simon. Max, who had brought his friend Henry, who had brought Darcy. Cara, who had brought Camilla, who had brought Paris. Billy, who had brought Brittany, who had brought Bono with his new headbanging CD. Anoushka and Liberty came together and brought their friends David and Matthew and then, of course, Chantelle, who brought all eight of her brothers, who didn't happen to mention their names. So, including Bronte, Trevor, Rudy and Ugenia that made a dinner party for twenty-nine people. Sebastian and Lara couldn't make it.

'Welcome to our world!' announced Rudy, who offered everyone a glass of tarberry juice and before he even had time to have a seat the dinner party was in full swing.

Sita, Simon and Sandra were hoovering down the pineapples and Liberty was flicking olives. Camilla, Cara and Paris began slapping slices of ham on each other's foreheads. Brittany, Billy and Bono began playing frisbee with the macaroons and shoving the parsnips up each other's noses.

David and Matthew were dancing around in Ugenia's mother's clothes. Anoushka began making an extremely marvellous modern punch and popped it in the oven. Then Chantelle and her eight brothers began throwing ice-cream sandwiches at each other and diving off the sofa as they shouted along to Bono's new headbanging CD.

'FOOD FIGHT!' screamed Camilla.

'Get 'em,' shouted Chantelle.

'Take that!'

'TAKE THIS,' yelled Max, shoving ice
cream in Anoushka's face.

Suddenly, Ugenia's house was in chaos
– a food war zone. The entire contents of
the table was now either splattered across
the living room, all over Ugenia's mother's

best ornaments and lampshades, or shoved in someone's hair. Billy and Bono swung from the curtains, doing their best ape impressions. Ugenia watched in horror as Chantelle's brothers swiped her mother's most precious porcelain ancient-tribal-statue headpiece and threw it across the room. Ugenia screamed as it flew through the air and landed on a beanbag, narrowly missing Bronte's head.

'Oh, Ugenia, this is getting out of control,' cried Bronte.

'Oh, Rudy, what are we gonna do?' cried Ugenia.

149

'Trevor, help!
Do something!'
screamed Rudy.

'STOP IT
RIGHT NOW!'
shouted Trevor in a
very loud, deep, scary voice as he turned
off the headbanging music. Everyone
froze in amazement and slowly put down
whatever it was they were about to throw.

'AND GET OUT NOW!' said Trevor
firmly, who suddenly looked older than
nine, with his arms firmly crossing his chest
like he was a bouncer standing outside a
nightclub.

Slowly, Sita, Simon, Sandra, Max,
Henry, Darcy, Camilla, Cara, Paris,
Brittany, Billy, Bono, David, Matthew,

Anoushka, Liberty, Chantelle and her eight brothers all brushed themselves off and left the Lavender house with their heads hanging in shame.

'Well, that certainly told them, didn't it?' beamed Rudy.

'Trevor, you were wonderful! Thank you,' smiled Ugenia.

'Very nice,' said Bronte.

'Er . . . no problem' said Trevor, and suddenly the telephone rang.

'Er, hello?' said Ugenia.

'Hello, darling, it's Mum. Is everything OK?' said Pandora.

'Yes, fine!' Ugenia squirmed as she stared at the food explosion in the living room.

'Everything is under control, just relax, get better, don't worry about a thing,' she said as she began to smell something very odd coming from the kitchen. Suddenly there was an almighty bang from the oven.

'Anoushka's extremely marvellous modern punch!' gasped Ugenia.

'What was that?' asked her mum.

'Er, nothing,' said Ugenia as she stared into the kitchen, which was splattered in tarberry juice. 'It's probably just Uncle Harry working on some new recipe! Mum, I've got to go, he needs me, mustn't keep him waiting, get well soon.'

'Phew, that was a close one,' Rudy sighed as Ugenia slammed down the phone.

'Rudy, this house is such a wreck,' said Ugenia. 'What am I going to do?' But before they had time to make another plan, the front doorbell rang. It was Ugenia's Granny Betty.

Granny Betty wandered into the living room and gasped, 'Mother dear goodness, you've been burgled! The vandals! We must call the police, you poor children!'

And before Ugenia could explain, Granny Betty was dialling 999. As quick as you could say, 'Oh, what a disaster,' the sound of the familiar sirens came gushing into Cromer Road and a very large white van appeared. A surge of police in full combat gear came running into Ugenia's living room.

'Well, officers, quite frankly you're too late, you should be ashamed of yourselves,' snapped Granny Betty. 'Where were you when these poor defenceless children needed your help? I think the best thing you can do is clean up.'

Granny Betty handed the officers mops
and buckets, dishcloths and a vacuum
cleaner.

'Er, sorry, ma'am, yes of course,' they
said in unison.

The twelve police officers meekly went
down on their hands and knees and got

straight to work, polishing the ornaments and hoovering the carpet. Ugenia decided the best thing to do was to put the kettle on and pretend it was all going to be OK (after all, wasn't that what grown-ups did? Right?).

'Many hands make light work!' giggled Granny Betty, who offered everyone some Christmas cake (even though it definitely was not Christmas).

An hour later, the house was back in perfect, sparkling shape. The twelve policemen, Rudy, Trevor and Bronte said their goodbyes and went home.

Ugenia looked at Granny. 'Gran, being a grown-up is hard work,' she announced, suddenly beginning to feel exhausted.

'Tell me about it!' smiled Granny Betty.

Then, suddenly, the doorbell rang. It was Uncle Harry. 'I can't work with those incredible imbeciles. I decided not to go,' he shouted. 'I'm taking some time off. Shall I make us some incredible salmon soufflés with broccoli, and pineapple fritters for afters?'

'Great!' smiled Ugenia, who was delighted that a real grown-up was back (Granny Betty didn't really count, even if she was 101).

Suddenly, the front doorbell rang again. This time it was Doctor Clooney, followed by Pandora and Edward Lavender bandaged up and on crutches.

'Surprise!' said Ugenia's mother. 'We couldn't stand the thought of you all by yourself with just Uncle Harry, so we thought we'd come and recover with you in the comfort of our own lovely home.'

Ugenia threw her arms around her mum and dad and gave them a hug. 'It's so good to see you.'

'Now, Ugenia, was everything all right?' asked Professor Lavender, hobbling around.

'The house looks very clean,' smiled Pandora. 'You've been cleaning up. Thank you, you've really shown us what a thoughtful, responsible, grown up young lady you really are!'

Then, suddenly, Ugenia's mother seemed to notice something out of the corner of her eye. It was her most precious porcelain ancient-tribal-statue headpiece.

'Ugenia, just one question, what on earth is a parsnip doing shoved up my porcelain

statue's nose?' she cried.

'Er . . . it likes parsnips?'
smiled Ugenia.

Big News!

Hello ello ello!
Oh, crikey, that got a bit out of control! If you're as confused as I am, I don't blame you – I mean Granny Betty calling the police! How mad is that? Although they did a great clean-up job!

And Trevor really came

through. Actually, everyone did
– even Colleen in the supermarket
was kind to me – you really find
out who your friends are when
you're in BIG trouble.

Anyway, my mum found out
that I had had some dinner guests
over – there was some ham still
stuck on the ceiling, that the
policemen missed – so I came
clean about my best intentions to
be all grown up! Actually, being a
grown-up is definitely overrated,
believe me!

What else, oh, my mum looks
beautiful again – the bandages are
off and she is back on Breakfast

TV with her new slot, and the boss likes her, so she is feeling less snappy. And Dad, well, he is still on crutches but is hobbling to the dino museum. He actually wants to go back to Kathmandu — wherever that is — to get my mum another statue.

OK, I've got to run.

Big XO

Ugenia Lavender XX

Ingenious Top Tip

Until you've walked a mile in my shoes, don't tell me how to walk it

Look, I had no idea how hard it is being a grown-up until I experienced it for half a day. Now I feel a little bit more sympathetic to my mum's moaning!

Brain
Squeezers

Ugenia's Incredible Quiz

Incredible things just seem to happen to me all the time! But how much can you remember about them? Try my fun quiz to see if you're a Ugenia expert.

1. Rudy and his family invited me on holiday with them, but I had to go to Lamorca instead. Where did *they* go?

- ☑ India
- ☐ Africa
- ☐ China

2. According to my dad, Professor Lavender, what kind of dinosaur was first discovered on the island of Lamorca?

- ☐ Tyrannosaurus rex
- ☐ Sillysaurus rex
- ☑ Gorillasaurus rex

3. I entered a competition to win a VIP pass to the Lunar Park Funfair – but I won something I didn't want instead. What was it?

☐ A blue shiny bag
☑ A red plastic purse
☐ A glittery gold pencil

4. Oh no! My dinner party went horribly wrong when my guests started a major food fight. Which of my friends stepped in and put an end to it?

☑ Trevor
☐ Rudy
☐ Bronte

5. What colour is my rucksack (the one I take everywhere with me)?

☐ Fluorescent pink
☑ Luminous yellow
☐ Bright orange

Ugenia's Dinner Party Shopping Snake

When I was home alone I invited all my friends over for a stylish dinner party! Here are some of the things I bought for it. Can you find the words below on the grid – they go in one continuous line, snaking upwards, downwards, backwards and forwards, but *never* diagonally. The words are in the same order as the list.

ICE CREAM

PARSNIPS

OLIVES

HAM

PINEAPPLE

POPCORN

MACAROONS

Tip! Use a pencil in case you make a mistake. Then you can just start again!

Start here

```
I  C  E  S     N
E  R  C  O     O
A  M  P  R     A
S  R  A  A     C
N  S  O  M     N
I  P  L  O     R
E  V  I  C     P
S  H  E  P     O
M  A  L  P     P
P  I  N  E     A
```

Ugenia's Holiday Crossword

I ended up having a great time in Lamorca, staying at the hotel with the aqua-aerobics, karaoke, fish buffet and everything. If you love holidays too, try completing my holiday crossword!

ACROSS

1. When you fly on a plane, you have to wear a seat _ _ _ _.

2. If you're going away, you'll need to pack all your bits and pieces in one of these. Don't forget to put a luggage label on it!

4. A piece of land surrounded by water. If you get stuck on one of these, try sending a message in a bottle.

DOWN

1. When I'm on holiday I love to relax here. It's got golden sand, blue water and, if you're lucky, sunloungers and ice cream!

2. Time to get some exercise – let's jump into the pool and get _ _ _ _ _ _ _ _.

3. If you're travelling to a far-off destination, you'll be flying in one of these. Prepare for take-off!

Ugenia's Funfair Food

One of the best things about funfairs is all the yummy snacks you can buy! Probably best not to eat all these and then go on the 'Death Wish' ride though . . . bleeugh! Can you match up these mouth-watering snacks by drawing lines to the correct word?

candy   burger

hot   apple

ice   floss

milk   cream

cheese   shake

toffee   dog

Ugenia's Incredible Quiz

1. India
2. Gorillasaurus rex
3. A red plastic purse
4. Trevor
5. Luminous yellow

Ugenia's Dinner Party Shopping Snake

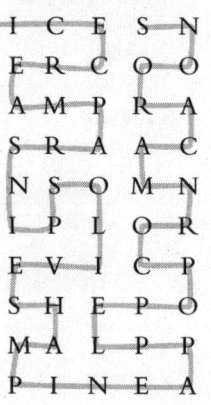

```
I C E S N
E R C O O
A M P R A
S R A A C
N S O M N
I P L O R
E V I C P
S H E P O
M A L P P
P I N E A
```

Ugenia's Holiday Crossword

ACROSS
1. Belt
2. Suitcase
4. Island

DOWN
1. Beach
2. Swimming
3. Plane

Ugenia's Funfair Food

candy – floss
hot – dog
ice – cream
milk – shake
cheese – burger
toffee – apple

Answers!

Ugenia Lavender is moving to 13 Cromer Road. How will she fit in as the new girl at school? Does she ever discover the meaning of the Lovely Illness? And can she rescue celebrity chef Uncle Harry from a big mix-up?

Ugenia Lavender

and the Terrible Tiger

When Ugenia Lavender meets Elsa at the
travelling circus, can she prove that the
terrible tiger is more of a purring pussycat?
And how will she stop arch-enemy Lara
Slater from being a Leading Lady Thief?
Does Ugenia stay the most popular girl
in the school? Or will it be more a case of
Ugenia Lavender, Who Do U Think U R?

UGenia Lavender

and the Burning Pants

The school sports day is fast approaching
and everyone wants to win a trophy. But
then Ugenia Lavender's birthday falls on
Friday the thirteenth, and things start to go
from bad to worse. Will a pair of burning
pants help Ugenia stop her best friend's
mum from marrying the wrong person?
And can Ugenia show her friends that it's
the taking part that counts, but still end up
with a prize?

Ugenia Lavender

and the Temple of Gloom

Ugenia is convinced there is a real live giant
living next door to her Granny Betty. But
just how does she prove it? And can she
stop her parents from being taken in by a
beautiful bloodsucker? Just as Ugenia thinks
it can't get any worse she finds herself stuck
in the Temple of Gloom. Will she ever find a
way out?

uGenia Lavender

The One and Only

Ugenia Lavender has discovered that the planet is fast running out of energy. But luckily she has a plan to save the day. How can she help an alien return to outer space? And what happens when she meets her hero, Hunk Roberts? Does it make up for the fact that Ugenia might no longer be the One and Only?

Incredible praise for Ugenia Lavender!

'You know Geri the Spice Girl, now meet Geri the author!' *Sun*

'[A] lovable heroine' *Sunday Express*

'It's inspirational! It's totally ingenious!' *Independent on Sunday*

'[Geri] has created a heroine who is strong, sassy, believable . . .' *Mail on Sunday*

'Be enchanted by Geri Halliwell's children's book, *Ugenia Lavender*' *Daily Express*

A selected list of titles available from Macmillan Children's Books

The prices shown below are correct at the time of going to press. However, Macmillan Publishers reserves the right to show new retail prices on covers, which may differ from those previously advertised.

Geri Halliwell

Ugenia Lavender	978-0-330-45425-4	£4.99
Ugenia Lavender and the Terrible Tiger	978-0-330-45429-2	£4.99
Ugenia Lavender and the Burning Pants	978-0-330-45430-8	£4.99
Ugenia Lavender: Home Alone	978-0-330-45431-5	£4.99
Ugenia Lavender and the Temple of Gloom	978-0-330-45432-2	£4.99
Ugenia Lavender: The One and Only	978-0-330-45433-9	£4.99

All Pan Macmillan titles can be ordered from our website, www.panmacmillan.com, or from your local bookshop and are also available by post from:

Bookpost, PO Box 29, Douglas, Isle of Man IM99 1BQ
Credit cards accepted. For details:
Telephone: 01624 677237
Fax: 01624 670923
Email: bookshop@enterprise.net
www.bookpost.co.uk

Free postage and packing in the United Kingdom